WAY OF THE RAT

The Walls
of Zhumar

Publisher's Cataloging in Publication Data
(Prepared by The Donohue Group, Inc.)

Way of the rat. Volume one : The Walls of Zhumar / Writer: Chuck Dixon ; Penciler: Jeff Johnson ; Inker: Tom
Ryder ; Colorist: Chris Garcia.

p. : ill. ; cm.

Spine title: Way of the rat. 1 : the walls of Zhumar

ISBN: 1-931484-51-1

1. Fantasy Fiction. 2. Adventure fiction. 3. Graphic novels. 4. Boon Sai Hong (Fictitious character)--Fiction. 5.
Po Po (Fictitious character)--Fiction. I. Dixon, Chuck, 1954- II. Johnson, Jeff. III. Ryder, Tom. IV. Garcia, Chris.
V. Title: Walls of Zhumar VI. Title: Way of the rat. 1 : the walls of Zhumar.

PN6728 .W39 2002
813.54 [Fic]

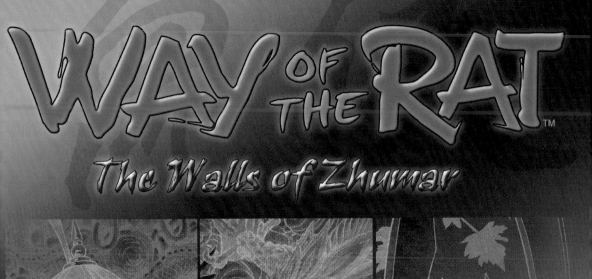

WAY OF THE RAT

The Walls of Zhumar

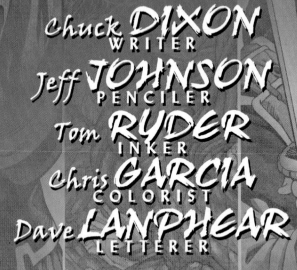

Chuck **DIXON**
WRITER

Jeff **JOHNSON**
PENCILER

Tom **RYDER**
INKER

Chris **GARCIA**
COLORIST

Dave **LANPHEAR**
LETTERER

CHAPTER 5

Rod **WHIGHAM** · PENCILER
Drew **GERACI** · INKER

CrossGeneration Comics   **Oldsmar, Florida**

The Walls of Zhumar

features
Chapters 1-6
from the ongoing series

WAY OF THE RAT

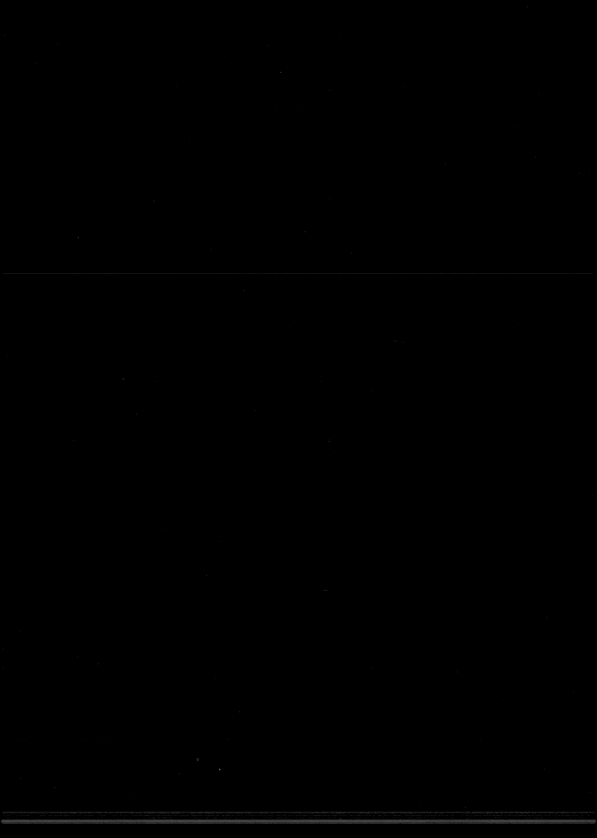

"It is the wise man
who can discern
good fortune from ill."

Wing Tei Sun

THE FRONTIER CITY OF ZHUMAR, FAR TO THE WEST OF THE COMFORTS AND PLEASURES OF THE IMPERIAL COURT.

A FORTRESS BUILT HARD BY THE ENDLESS STEPPES.

HOME TO ONE HUNDRED THOUSAND HAPLESS SOULS WHO LIVE EACH DAY BENEATH THE SHADOW OF A TARTAR'S SWORD.

YOU HAVE PROMISED MY MASTER THE RING OF STAFFS. I HAVE BEEN HERE *THREE* DAYS AND MY HANDS ARE EMPTY.

IT IS *WITHIN* MY GRASP. I HOPE YOUR KHAN RECALLS *HIS* PROMISES AS WELL AS YOU DO *MINE*.

THE DEAL YOU STRUCK WITH HIM IS *MEANINGLESS* WITHOUT THE RING TO SEAL IT.

IT *WILL* BE HERE. I HAVE SENT MY BEST MEN TO RETRIEVE IT. ONLY THE LIFE OF A FEEBLE *BOOKWORM* STANDS IN MY WAY.

I *TOLD* YOU...

SHOULD HE BE DISAPPOINTED, THE KHAN'S *WRATH* IS AS GREAT AS HIS GENEROSITY.

Eh?

AND?

VENERABLE JUSTICE -- I HAVE COME FROM THE HOME OF THE SCHOLAR WING TEI.

WE *FAILED* TO OBTAIN THE RING. *PRINCESS ZHENG* WAS THERE AND—

AND A *THIEF* -- HE STOLE THE RING AND ESCAPED.

ZHENG MAI? THAT *WITCH*?

I WOULD DO *ANYTHING* TO EXPUNGE MY SHAME.

DID YOU *HEAR* THAT, NUBOTAI?

I *DID*, JUDGE.

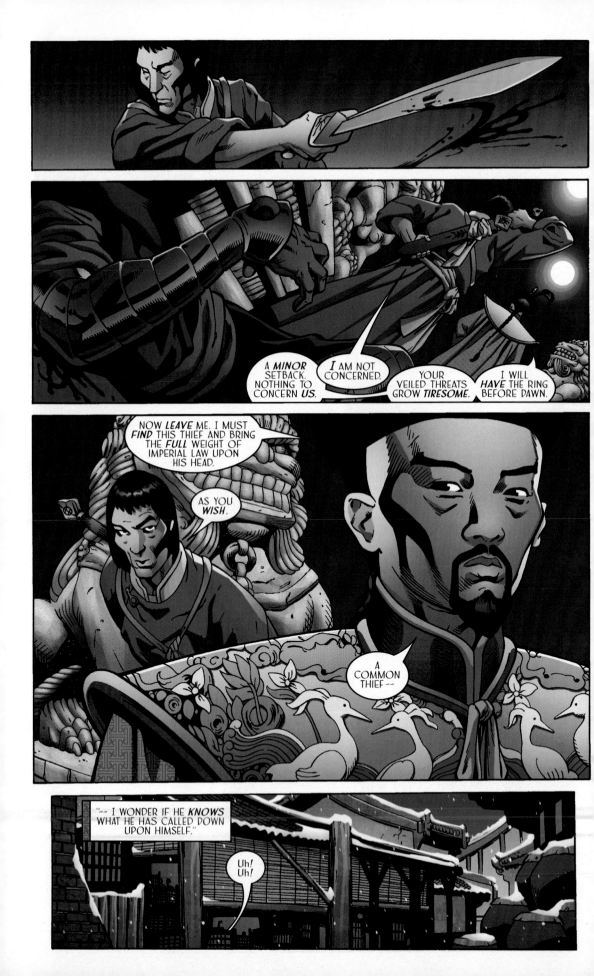

"Run from one fate only to run to another. Better to chance destiny's winds than to break against them." Wing Tei Sun

"For all of our fine ways we are in danger.
For all our virtues there is a weakness.
For every dream there is a danger."

from *Principles of Civilization* by Wing Tei Sun

"Outside of our temples and palaces and libraries are those who care nothing for our fine art and writing and thought.

"To the South the Ghilzais.

"To the East the armies of Nayado's emperor.

"To the West the Devil's own horsemen.

"Limitless in ferocity and number. Infinite in cruelty. They wait like hunting wolves for a sign of frailty or moment of inattention."

"Be forever watchful. Should one come to forge the tribes into a killing wind from the West, that will be the last of our days."

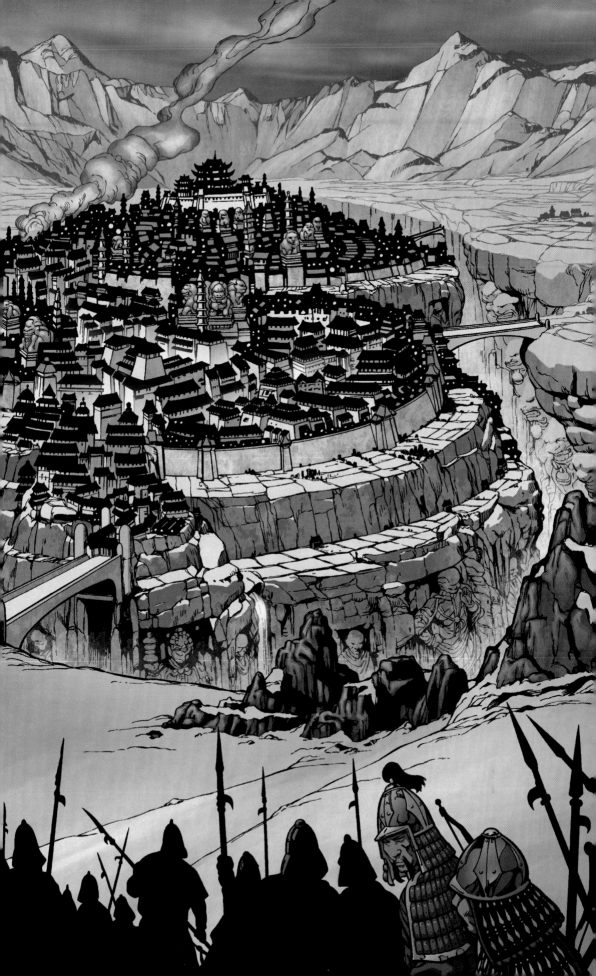

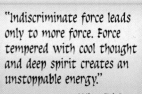

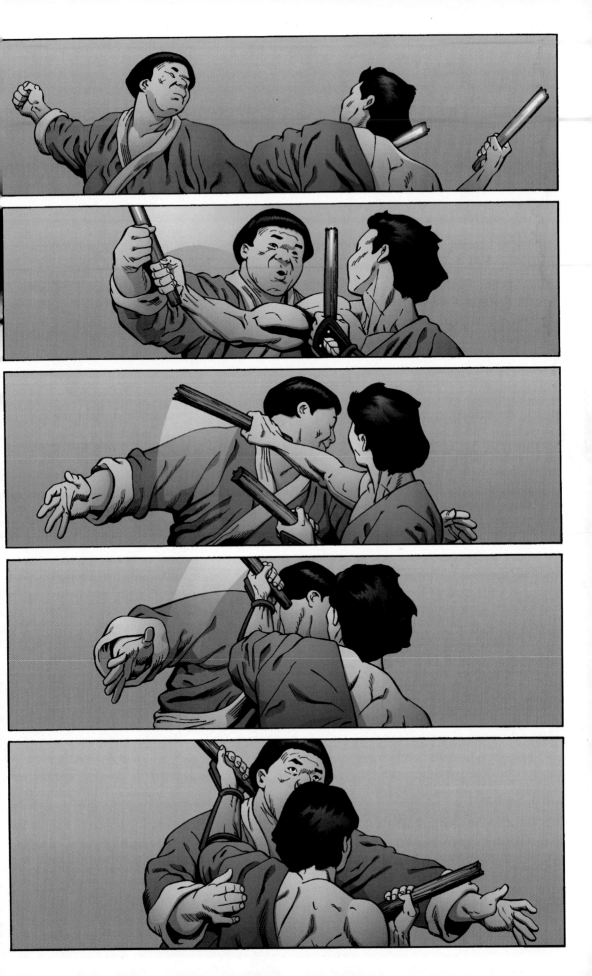

"WORKERS WERE TAKEN TO THE EASTERN WALL AND SET TO THE TASK.

"THE DRIFTS *GREW* EVEN AS THEY REMOVED THEM.

"EVEN WORSE WERE THE ARROWS OF BHUTO KHAN.

"AFTER THAT EVEN THE THREAT OF *BLINDING* COULD NOT FORCE THE LABORERS THROUGH THE GATE."

"WINTER HAS SO
LONG BEEN OUR
ALLY, CLOAKING US
FROM THE DANGERS
WITHOUT.

"FOR A FEW FROZEN
MONTHS WE WERE
SAFE FROM HARM.

"BUT WITH THIS
SEASON'S SNOW
CAME THE
HORSEMEN."

"To my enemies I say,
May you live in
interesting times."

Wing Tei Sun

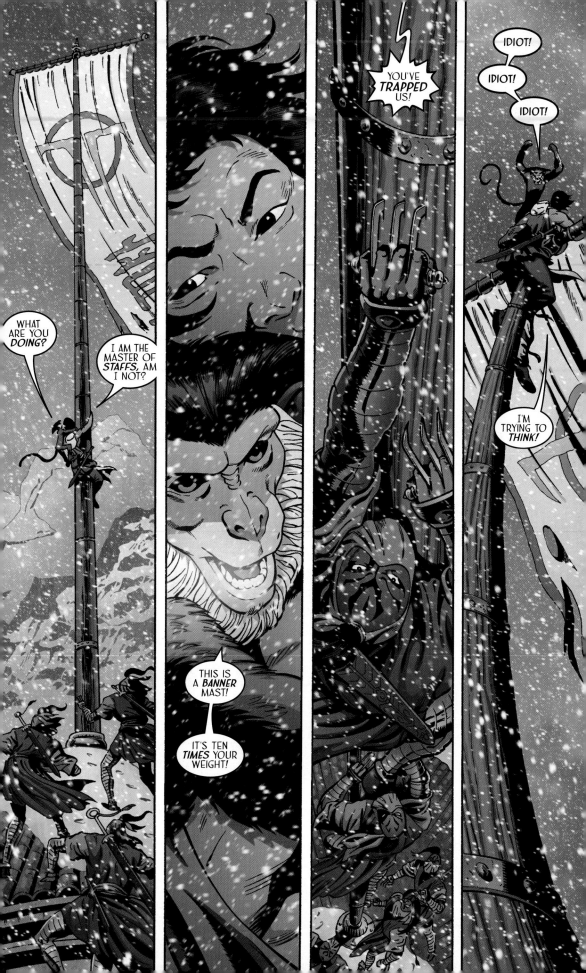

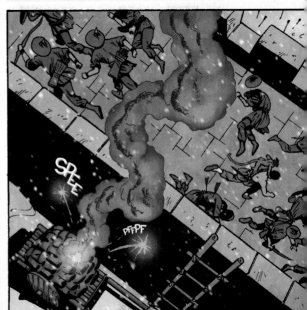

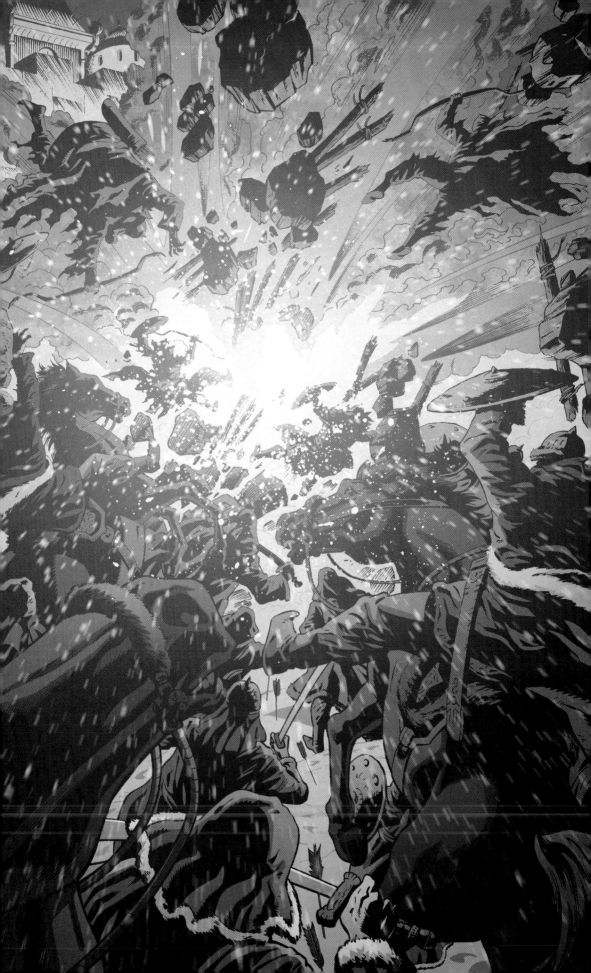